METROPOLITAN COW

Written and Illustrated by Tim Egan

HOUGHTON MIFFLIN COMPANY

BOSTON

For Mom and Dad

The text of this book is set in 16-point Dante.
The illustrations are watercolor and ink, reproduced in full color.

LIBRARY OF CONGRESS CATALOGING-IN-PUBLICATION DATA
Egan, Tim.
Metropolitan cow / Tim Egan.
p. cm.
Summary: Although Bennett's parents, who are very cosmopolitan cows,
are uncomfortable with the idea, Bennett becomes good friends with Webster,
a young pig who moves in next door.
RNF ISBN 0-395-73096-1 PAP ISBN 0-395-96059-2
[1. Cows — Fiction. 2. Pigs — Fiction. 3. Friendship — Fiction.]
I. Title   PZ7.F2815ME 1996   [E]—dc20
95-23382   CIP   AC

Manufactured in the United States of America
BVG 10 9 8 7 6 5 4

$\mathcal{B}ennett$ $\mathcal{G}ibbons$ was a very fortunate young cow. His parents, Frederick and Henrietta, were prominent members of their herd and noted socialites. They lived in a beautiful apartment and gave Bennett just about everything he could want.

Indeed, young Bennett Gibbons was the luckiest little calf in the neighborhood. Problem was, he was also the *only* little calf in the neighborhood.

Oh, there were other cows around. And Bennett would sometimes go to the park and watch them play croquet, but they were quite a bit older than he was. He also liked watching the pigs slosh around in the mud, but they were older, too. Besides, cows didn't play with pigs.

One afternoon, Bennett asked his mom, "Can I go jump in the mud? It looks like fun."

"Don't be ridiculous, Bennett," she said. "You know cows don't go in the mud. That's for the pigs. We're far too dignified for such nonsense."

The next day, as he sat playing in his room, Bennett heard a noise in the hallway. He looked out and saw a family of pigs moving in next door. Being the polite young cow that he was, he introduced himself. "Hello," he said. "I'm Bennett Gibbons."

"Well, hello there," said the mother pig. "We're the Andersons. We just moved here from the country. This is our son, Webster." Bennett and Webster looked at each other. They both said "Hi" at the same time. Webster seemed like a nice pig.

Bennett and Webster were about the same age, and they became friends that very afternoon. The next day, Bennett asked his father, "Can I show Webster around the neighborhood a little? It's okay with his dad if it's okay with you."

Bennett's father raised his eyebrow and said, "Frankly, Bennett, it's a little unusual for a cow to be playing with a pig, but I suppose it's all right for today. Just be back before dark." And off they went.

As they ran down the stairs, Webster said, "Hey, let's go jump in the mud!"

"No, I can't," said Bennett. "I'm too dignified."

"What does that mean?" asked Webster.

"I have no idea," replied Bennett.

Instead, they went to Bennett's favorite place, the Natural History Museum. Webster was speechless when he saw the giant brachiosaurus exhibit, and he was equally impressed with the sleek-looking escalator.

Next, they went to see a movie. It was supposed to be really funny, but they both agreed it wasn't. As they left the theater, Webster said, "I don't mean to be critical, but that was the dumbest movie I've ever seen."

"I absolutely agree," said Bennett, "though I did enjoy the buttered popcorn."

"Indeed," said Webster, "not to mention the chocolate-covered mints."

A while later, they stopped to eat pretzels on the street corner. Webster asked Bennett, "Have you ever tried whistling while eating a pretzel? It's almost impossible."

"I don't know how to whistle," confessed Bennett. So Webster spent the next twenty minutes teaching Bennett the fine art of whistling. Bennett was very grateful. Then they both tried whistling with pretzels in their mouths. They couldn't.

As the days passed, Mr. and Mrs. Gibbons seemed a little uncomfortable with Bennett's new friendship. They liked young Webster, but he was, after all, a pig. And pigs seemed so unsophisticated to them—the way they'd roll around in the mud and make those strange oinking sounds.

But none of that mattered to Bennett. He and Webster were too busy playing checkers and building houses out of cards. It took great patience, but they built one that was ten stories high before it fell.

Then, one evening in the park, while Bennett and Webster were getting rambunctious, the unthinkable happened. Bennett, in a moment of pure recklessness, ran across the grass and jumped in the mud. It was much warmer than he'd expected. It was also, needless to say, a shock to everyone.

"Bennett!" yelled his father. "You come out of there right now! Show some dignity!"

His mother shouted, "Bennett Gibbons! We've put up with this nonsense long enough! I don't think you should play with that pig anymore!"

Bennett jumped out of the mud and yelled, "That's not fair!" and took off down the street.

"Bennett!" yelled his father. "Come back here!" But Bennett was a fast little cow and was already gone.

Webster looked up at his dad and said, "We've got to help find him. He's my best friend." Without saying a word, the Gibbonses and the Andersons started down the street.

They went through the alley and around the library, but there was no sign of Bennett. Then they searched down by the hotel and near the bookstore, but he wasn't there either. It was getting dark.

"Oh, Frederick," said Mrs. Gibbons. "What have we done? Where could he be? How will we ever find him in this big city?"

"I don't know, Henrietta," Mr. Gibbons said dramatically. "I just don't know."

Then, just as Mrs. Gibbons started crying, Webster said, "Wait. I bet I know where he is." He started running and they all followed him.

They ran about a half mile, and sure enough, there was Bennett, sitting on the steps of the Natural History Museum, his favorite place. As his mother ran toward him, he said, "I guess I shouldn't have run away, but if having dignity means I can't play with Webster, then I don't want any. He's my best friend."

"Well, Bennett," said Mrs. Gibbons, "he's our friend, too. In fact, he's the one who knew where to find you."

"That he did," said Mr. Gibbons. "And if his parents can forgive us for being such fools, you can play with him all you want."

Fortunately for everyone, the Andersons were very forgiving pigs, and they all headed home.

As they walked along, they realized how very much alike they were. They liked the same music and the same books. They enjoyed the same movies. And they all were vegetarians.

As they passed the park, Bennett said, "I guess I can't go in the mud anymore, right?"

"No, Bennett, you may not," his father said sternly. "At least not before I do!" And then he, like his son before him, ran across the grass and jumped in the mud. It was warmer than he'd expected, too.

Everyone howled with laughter, and seconds later, Mr. Anderson jumped in. Then Webster. And finally, with great satisfaction, Bennett.

Mrs. Anderson and Mrs. Gibbons didn't want to ruin their dresses so they just sat on the side, but you could see that they, too, had become good friends.